DOG ON A BROOMSTICK

JAN PAGE

Illustrated by Nick Price

For My Mother

DOG ON A BROOMSTICK
A CORGI BOOK 978 0 552 56900 2

Published in Great Britain by Corgi Books,
an imprint of Random House Children's Publishers UK
A Random House Group Company

Corgi Pups edition published 1997
This Colour First Reader edition published 2013

1 3 5 7 9 10 8 6 4 2

The Random House Group Limited supports the Forest Stewardship Council (FSC®),
the leading international forest certification organization. Our books carrying the FSC
label are printed on FSC®-certified paper. FSC is the only forest certification scheme
endorsed by the leading environmental organizations, including Greenpeace. Our paper
procurement policy can be found at www.randomhouse.co.uk/environment.

Set in Bembo MT Schoolbook 21/28pt

Corgi Books are published by Random House Children's Publishers UK,
61–63 Uxbridge Road, London W5 5SA

www.**randomhousechildrens**.co.uk
www.**randomhouse**.co.uk

Addresses for companies within The Random House Group Limited can be found at:
www.randomhouse.co.uk/offices.htm

THE RANDOM HOUSE GROUP Limited Reg. No. 954009

A CIP catalogue record for this book is available from the British Library.

Printed in Italy.

Contents

COLOUR FIRST READER books are perfect for beginner readers. All the text inside this Colour First Reader book has been checked and approved by a reading specialist, so it is the ideal size, length and level for children learning to read.

Series Reading Consultant: Prue Goodwin
Honorary Fellow of the University of Reading

Chapter One

The Witch woke up one night to find her cat had gone. It had left a note on the cat flap.

"I have given up magic," the note read. "I have found a new job, testing cat food."

The Witch was very cross.

She needed a cat to help her with her spells. And there were only three days to go until the Grand Spell Contest!

"Bother! I'll have to find a
new cat," she said.

In the morning, the Witch put
on her tallest hat and went to the
pet shop.

"I want to buy a cat," she told
the shop-keeper.

The shop-keeper did not like the look of the Witch, but he showed her some black kittens in a basket.

"Do they scratch?" asked the Witch.

"No!" said the shop-keeper.

"Do they arch their backs?"

"No!" said the shop-keeper.

"Do they spit and hiss?"

"No!" said the shop-keeper.
"Never!"

"What a shame," said the Witch
and walked out of the shop.

Next, the Witch went to the
RSPCA. There were lots of cats
there, all looking for a new home.

The Witch made them sit in a row and told them about the job.

"I am looking for a cat to help me with my spells," she said. "You will have to catch mice, spiders and worms. And sometimes, I might turn you into a frog. Any questions?"

A fat white cat raised her paw. "Will we have to fly on your broomstick?"

"Of course!" said the Witch.

"I don't fancy that," said the fat white cat. "I get airsick."

"Hopeless!" cried the Witch. She went to see the lady in charge.

"None of these cats are any good," she told her. "They are not

lean enough. They are not mean
enough. And their eyes are not
green enough!"

"If I found you the right cat,
would you promise to look after
it?" asked the lady.

"Of course not!" said the Witch.
"I want a cat so that it can look
after me!"

The Witch walked out in a temper. Where was she going to find a cat in time for the Grand Spell Contest?

Chapter Two

On her way home the Witch
went to buy some black
chocolates. This gave her a good
idea.

"I know! I'll put a card in the shop window."

The Witch wrote out the words and gave them to the shop-keeper.

Wanted —
Witch's Cat!
Must be able to scratch, hiss and spit.
Only black cats with green eyes need apply.

"That should do it," she said.

The Witch went home and waited. She waited all day and all night but not one cat came.

She was in a panic. Now it was
only two days until the Grand
Spell Contest.

Then, on Thursday evening
there was a scratch at the door.

"At last!" she cried.

She opened the door and saw
a dog sitting on the doorstep.

"Bother!" said the Witch.

"I was hoping you had come about the job."

"I have come about the job," said the Dog.

"But this job is for a cat!" said the Witch.

"That's a bit unfair," replied the Dog. "I am sure I could

do the job just as well . . . if not
better."

"Don't be stupid!" cried the
Witch. "Witches don't have dogs.

Who ever heard of a Witch's dog?"
But the Dog was not giving up.

"I can fetch and carry. I can hunt. I can bark at strange people."

"But I like strange people," said the Witch. "A lot of my friends are strange people!"

"I will always do as I am told. I will be the perfect witch's dog. Please let me try!"

The Dog sat on the doorstep and wagged his tail. He really wanted this job. He was so hungry and cold, he didn't care

what he had to do to find a new
home.

The Witch looked him up and
down.

"Can you miaow?" she asked.

"No . . . but I can howl at the
moon," said the Dog. He opened
his mouth and let out a loud, wild
howl.

"Ooh, I like that! That sounds
very scary!" The Witch smiled and
showed her black, crooked teeth.

"Can you hiss and spit?" asked
the Witch.

"No . . . but I can growl and
dribble," said the Dog. He gave a
deep growl and dribbled all over
the floor.

"Very good! What a lovely mess! . . . Now, can you arch your back and make your fur stand on end?"

"No . . . but I can roll over and leave hair all over the carpet," said the Dog. He showed her his best roll.

"That hair could come in
handy for my spells," said the
Witch, feeling very pleased.
"Now I want you to catch a
mouse."

The Dog did not know how
to catch mice. He found a toy
mouse in the old cat's basket
and put it between his teeth. The
Witch didn't seem to notice.

"Good! Pop it in the cauldron!
. . . Now fetch me some worms
from the garden. Fat ones, or the
spell won't work."

The Dog ran into the garden
and dug a hole. He soon came
back with the fattest worms the
Witch had ever seen.

"Now sit still while I try out this spell on you."

The Dog sat very still.

"Squeak of mice. Croak of frog. You will turn into a dog!"

"But I am a dog," said the Dog quietly, not wishing to make the Witch cross.

"Oh yes. Bother!"

"Try this instead," said the Dog. "Squeak of mice, bark of dog. You will turn into a frog!"

"Very good," croaked the Witch from under the cauldron.

The Dog had turned the
Witch into a frog, but she didn't
seem to mind too much.

They spent the night working on spells. Sometimes the Witch did spells on the Dog. Sometimes the Dog did spells on the Witch. She turned him into a banana, and

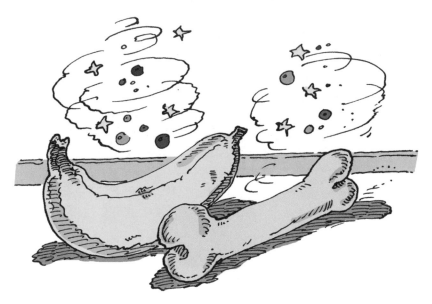

he turned her into a bone. Then she turned him into a carrot and he turned her into a donkey.

There was a nasty moment when
the donkey nearly ate the carrot.
But they had great fun all night.

"Now it's time for a ride on
my broomstick!" she cried.

"Can I come with you?" asked
the Dog. "I could do with the
fresh air."

So the dog sat on the end
of the Witch's broomstick and
she said the magic words. The
broomstick wobbled, but it could
not get off the ground.

"You're too heavy," said
the Witch. "That's why I
need a cat."

"Try again,
please!" begged
the Dog.

"Say
the spell
twice to
make it
stronger."
So the Witch
said the spell
twice and it worked.
The broomstick flew
up into the sky. The Dog
sat behind the Witch and howled
at the moon. He felt very happy.
His tail wagged so much he
almost fell off.

When they landed back in
the Witch's garden it was nearly
morning.

"Time for bed! We've a busy
night tomorrow," said the Witch.
"It's the Grand Spell Contest!"

"Does that mean I've got the
job?" asked the Dog.

"Of course!" cried the Witch.
"Just make sure you switch off the
cauldron before you go to bed."

Chapter Three

The Dog and the Witch slept for
most of the day. When it grew
dark the Dog woke up and went
into the garden. He rolled in the
mud and walked all over the
Witch's floor. Then he did lots of

dribbles and rubbed his fur into
the carpet. The place was such
a mess! He woke the Witch by
licking her hairy chin.

"Please," said the Dog. "Before
we go to the Spell Contest, could
you take me for a walk?"

"A walk? Why do you want to go for a walk?" asked the Witch as she got out of bed.

"All dogs need a walk," he
replied.

"Oh very well. I need to pop
into the woods to pick some
toadstools. But we must hurry!"

So the Witch took the Dog

and they went for a walk in the woods. While they were hunting for toadstools they met Witch Cackle and her cat Sooty. They were on their way to the Grand Spell Contest.

"What are you doing with that stupid dog?" asked Cackle.

"He's a witch's dog," said the Witch. The Dog growled and Sooty leapt up a tree.

"A witch's dog? There is no

such thing as a witch's dog!"

"Oh yes, there is. And I'm taking him to the Grand Spell Contest."

"You can't take a dog to the Grand Spell Contest! It's against the rules!"

"Is it?" said the Witch.

"Yes! It says so in the Rule Book. They will throw you out!" Cackle gave a horrible laugh. "Come along, Sooty, we must hurry!"

Sooty jumped on to Cackle's shoulder and the two of them rushed off.

"That's funny. I didn't know there were any rules for the Grand Spell Contest," said the Witch.

"I bet that witch is lying," said the Dog. "Come on, let's go."

"Oh no," said the Witch. "I
can't take you to the contest if
it's against the rules. Anyway, all
the other witches will laugh at
me. Cackle was right. There is no
such thing as a witch's dog."

The Witch took the Dog
home. She put on her tallest hat
and her long black gloves. She
picked up her spell-book and
a bag of worms for her spells.
The Dog watched her get ready,
feeling very sad.

"I'm very sorry, but you must
go," the Witch told the Dog.
"I'll have to get a cat
instead. Goodbye . . ."

"Goodbye," said the Dog. The
Witch got on her broomstick
and flew off to the Grand Spell
Contest. Tears ran down the
Dog's furry nose. Why couldn't
he be a witch's dog? Life was
very unfair!

Chapter Four

The Dog was very upset. He
had grown to love the Witch,
and he loved doing magic spells.
He did not want to go back to
living on the streets. It was warm

in the Witch's house with
the cauldron boiling away
all night. And she liked dirt and
mud around the place. It was the
perfect home for a dog ... But
he knew he had to go.

Then he saw something on the table. It was the Witch's wand! She had gone to the Grand Spell Contest without it.

"Oh no! She must have her wand!" cried the Dog. There was only one thing to do.

He put the wand in his mouth and ran off.

The Dog was glad the Witch never washed and was very smelly. He was able to follow her trail all the way to the Grand Spell Contest.

He arrived just in time. The
Witch was standing by the
cauldron, just about to do her
best spell.

"Hurry up!" cried the Bad
Fairy who was judging the
contest.

"Oh dear, oh dear," said the
Witch, looking in her bag and in
the pockets of her dress. "I have
forgotten my wand!"

All the other witches laughed at
her. "No cat, no wand! She's not a
real witch at all!" they shouted.

The Witch started to cry. Large
dirty tears rolled down her cheeks.
The witches laughed even more.

Then the Dog rushed in with the wand in his mouth. He dropped it at the Witch's feet.

"Thank you, thank you!" cried the Witch. "Now I can do my spell!"

"Wait!" said Cackle. "Stop the contest! Throw that witch out! Witch's dogs are against the rules!"

The other witches cheered and waved their wands.

"What rules?" said the Bad Fairy. "There are no rules!"

"See – I knew she was lying," said the Dog. He growled at Cackle and Sooty. All the other

witches' cats were terrified. They
ran into the wood and hid up the
trees.

"Come back!" shouted the
witches.

The Witch and her Dog did
their best spells. The Witch turned

the Dog into a banana and the
Dog turned the Witch into a
bone. The Witch turned the Dog
into a carrot and the Dog turned
the Witch into a donkey. The
carrot kept well away from the

donkey this time and everything
went perfectly.

None of the cats would come
down from the trees. So the other
witches had to do their spells
without any help. All the spells
went wrong, and Cackle did the

worst spell of all. The Bad Fairy
gave First Prize to the Witch
and her dog. It was a brand new
cauldron.

Just as the Witch was loading
her broomstick, Cackle came up.

"Where did you find that
witch's dog?" asked Cackle.

"That's my secret," said the
Witch.

"I was thinking, I might get a dog," said Cackle.

"Me too," said another witch.

"I fancy a black poodle," said another.

The Witch smiled at the Dog with her black, crooked teeth.

"Shall we go?" she said.

The broomstick was so heavy that it would not lift off the ground.

"Say the magic words three times to make the spell stronger," said the Dog.

So the Witch said the magic words three times and the broomstick flew into the sky. The Dog sat proudly behind the

Witch with the new cauldron
on his lap. He gave a loud, wild
howl at the moon. At last he had
a new home and a new job. And
there was no better job in the
world than being a witch's dog.

THE END

Colour First Readers

Welcome to Colour First Readers. The following pages are intended for any adults (parents, relatives, teachers) who may buy these books to share the stories with youngsters. The pages explain a little about the different stages of learning to read and offer some suggestions about how best to support children at a very important point in their reading development.

Children start to learn about reading as soon as someone reads a book aloud to them when they are babies. Book-loving babies grow into toddlers who enjoy sitting on a lap listening to a story, looking at pictures or joining in with familiar words. Young children who have listened to stories start school with an expectation of enjoyment from books and this positive outlook helps as they are taught to read in the more formal context of school.

Cracking the code

Before they can enjoy reading for and to themselves, all children have to learn how to crack the alphabetic code and make meaning out of the lines and squiggles we call letters and punctuation. Some lucky pupils find the process of learning to read undemanding; some find it very hard.

Most children, within two or three years, become confident at working out what is written on the page. During this time they will probably read collections of books which are graded; that is, the books introduce a few new words and increase in length, thus helping youngsters gradually to build up their growing ability to work out the words and understand basic meanings.

Eventually, children will reach a crucial point when, without any extra help, they can decode words in an entire book, albeit a short one. They then enter the next phase of becoming a reader.

Making meaning

It is essential, at this point, that children stop seeing progress as gradually 'climbing a ladder' of books of ever-increasing difficulty. There is a transition stage between building word recognition skills and enjoying reading a story. Up until now, success has depended on getting the words right but to get pleasure from reading to themselves, children need to fully comprehend the content of what they read. Comprehension will only be reached if focus is put on understanding meaning and that can only happen if the reader is not hesitant when decoding. At this fragile, transition stage, decoding should be so easy that it slowly becomes automatic. Reading a book with ease enables children to get lost in the story, to enjoy the unfolding narrative at the same time as perfecting their newly learned word recognition skills.

At this stage in their reading development, children need to:

- Practice their newly established early decoding skills at a level which eventually enables them to do it automatically

- Concentrate on making sensible meanings from the words they decode

- Develop their ability to understand when meanings are 'between the lines' and other use of literary language

- Be introduced, very gradually, to longer books in order to build up stamina as readers

In other words, new readers need books that are well within their reading ability and that offer easy encounters with humour, inference, plot-twists etc. In the past, there have been very few children's books that provided children with these vital experiences at an early stage. Indeed, some children had to leap from highly controlled teaching materials to junior novels.

This experience often led to reluctance in youngsters who were not yet confident enough to tackle longer books.

Matching the books to reading development

Colour First Readers fill the gap between early reading and children's literature and, in doing so, support inexperienced readers at a vital time in their reading development. Reading aloud to children continues to be very important even after children have learned to read and, as they are well written by popular children's authors, Colour First Readers are great to read aloud. The stories provide plenty of opportunities for adults to demonstrate different voices or expression and, in a short time, give lots to talk about and enjoy together.

Each book in the series combines a number of highly beneficial features, including:

- Well-written and enjoyable stories by popular children's authors

- Unthreatening amounts of print on a page

- Unrestricted but accessible vocabularies

- A wide interest age to suit the different ages at which children might reach the transition stage of reading development

- Different sorts of stories – traditional, set in the past, present or future, real life and fantasy, comic and serious, adventures, mysteries etc.

- A range of engaging illustrations by different illustrators

- Stories which are as good to read aloud to children as they are to be read alone

All in all, Colour First Readers are to be welcomed for children throughout the early primary school years – not only for learning to read but also as a series of good stories to be shared by everyone. I like to think that the word 'Readers' in the title of this series refers to the many young children who will enjoy these books on their journey to becoming lifelong bookworms.

Prue Goodwin
Honorary Fellow of the University of Reading

Helping children to enjoy *Dog on a Broomstick*

If a child can read a page or two fluently, without struggling with the words at all, then he/she should be able to read this book alone. However, children are all different and need different levels of support to help them become confident enough to read a book to themselves.

Some young readers will not need any help to get going; they can just get on with enjoying the story. Others may lack confidence and need help getting into the story. For these children, it may help if you talk about what might happen in the book. Explore the title, cover and first few illustrations with them, making comments and suggestions about any clues to what might happen in the story.

Read the first chapter aloud together. Don't make it a chore. If they are still reluctant to do it alone, read the whole book with them, making it an enjoyable experience. The following suggestions will not be necessary every time a book is read but, every so often, when a story has been particularly enjoyed, children love responding to it through creative activities.

Before reading

Dog on a Broomstick is a story about a witch. Before anyone starts to read, it may be a good idea to remind children about storybook witches – their cats, cauldrons, broomsticks, magic spells and most of all, that they are comic characters. Emphasise the humour in each episode of the tale.

During reading

Asking questions about a story can be really helpful to support understanding but don't ask too many – and don't make it feel like a test on what has happened. Relate the questions to the child's own experiences and imagination. For example, ask: 'What spell would you make?' or 'Don't you think it must be fun to keep changing things with your magic?'

Responding to the book

If your child has enjoyed this story, it increases the fun by doing something creative in response. If possible, provide art materials and dressing up clothes so that they can make things, play at being characters, write and draw, act out a scene or respond in some other way to the story.

Activities for children

If you have enjoyed reading this story, you could:

- Get a pencil, some paper and some colours to write and draw your favourite bit of the story.

- Look at the notes on pages 7 and 18 to find the words to fill the spaces in these sentences:

  1. The Witch's cat had got a new job testing ___ ____ .

  2. The cat had given up _____ .

  3. The Witch advertised for a cat that was _____ with _____ eyes.

  4. The new cat must be able to _____ , hiss and ____ .

- Find the bit of the story when the Witch asks the Dog these questions. What did the Dog say?

'Can you miaow?' 'No ... but _____?'

'Can you hiss and spit?' 'No ... but _____ ?'

- Ask a friend, or your mum, to play at making up a spell. You could pretend that a plastic bucket is your witch's cauldron; get some bits and pieces to put in the 'cauldron'; wave your pretend wand and make up some magic words to cast your spell.

- Draw and colour a big picture of the Witch and her Dog on a broomstick. (The illustration at the end of the story may help you.)

- Do the Cat and Dog true or false quiz:

  - **Dogs wag their tails when they are happy.**
    T or F

  - **'Woof woof' is a noise that a cat makes.**
    T or F

  - **Witches usually have cats as their pets.**
    T or F

  - **A baby dog is called a puppy.**
    T or F

ALSO AVAILABLE AS COLOUR FIRST READERS